Hansel and Gretel

retold by *Lisa Ingalls*

illustrated by *Laura Lydecker*

GT
PUBLISHING

NEW YORK

Text copyright © 1996, 1997 GT Publishing Corporation.
Illustrations copyright © 1996, 1997 Laura Lydecker.
Designed by Lara S. Demberg.
For information address GT Publishing Corporation,
16 East 40th Street, New York, New York 10016

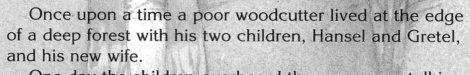

Once upon a time a poor woodcutter lived at the edge of a deep forest with his two children, Hansel and Gretel, and his new wife.

One day the children overheard the grown-ups talking.

"What will become of us?" moaned the husband. "The children are hungry and the cupboard is bare."

The woodcutter's wife had never liked Hansel or Gretel. She said, "I tell you, there is only one thing left to do. Tomorrow we must take the children into the forest and leave them there."

"No, no, I could never do that," protested the woodcutter. "Tomorrow I will leave home and look for work."

Hansel was worried by what his stepmother had said.
He suspected she would not give up her plan so easily.
That night, after everyone else had gone to sleep, he crept
outside. The white pebbles in the yard sparkled in the
moonlight. Hansel filled his pockets with the pebbles and
went back to bed.

The next morning, after the children had said good-bye
to their father, their stepmother led them off into the forest.
As they walked, Hansel stopped now and then to drop a
pebble on the ground.

When they had gone deep into the forest, the stepmother told the children to sit down and rest until she came back from gathering wood.

The stepmother was gone for a long while. Hansel and Gretel grew drowsy and fell asleep.

When they woke up, it was dark. Gretel began to cry, afraid they would never be able to find their way home.

"Wait until the moon comes out, Gretel," Hansel reassured her. "We will be able to see the white pebbles I dropped."

When the moon appeared, Hansel and Gretel followed the path of white pebbles all the way home.

The stepmother looked surprised to see them when she opened the door, but pretended that she had tried to find them. "I returned for you, but you must have wandered off," she said.

A few days later, the woodcutter's wife gave each of
the children a small piece of cheese for their lunch.
Then, she led them off into the forest again, even deeper
than before.

This time Hansel did not have a chance to fill his pockets
with pebbles. But as they walked along, he broke off little
bits of cheese and dropped them on the ground.

Once again the woodcutter's wife told the children to sit down and rest while she gathered wood. Once again Hansel and Gretel fell asleep and did not wake up until it was dark.

"Where's your cheese?" Gretel asked as she took hers out to eat.

"I used it to make a path," Hansel answered. So Gretel shared her cheese with her brother as the children waited for the moon to come up.

But when the moon appeared, Hansel and Gretel could not find the cheese trail. The birds and other animals had eaten it. This time Hansel and Gretel truly were lost.

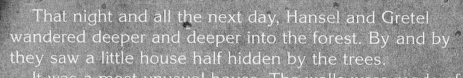

That night and all the next day, Hansel and Gretel
wandered deeper and deeper into the forest. By and by
they saw a little house half hidden by the trees.

It was a most unusual house. The walls were made of
gingerbread, and the windows of spun sugar. The roof was
covered with candies and little frosted cookies.

Hansel and Gretel were so hungry they immediately
started to eat. Hansel reached up and broke off a piece of
the roof and Gretel began to nibble at the windowsill.

An old woman appeared in the doorway. She said, "Nibble, nibble, little mouse, who's that nibbling at my house?"

The old woman hobbled up to the children. Her eyesight was failing, so she leaned forward, peering closely into their faces. She said, "Don't be afraid. I won't hurt you. Come into my house. There are even better things to eat inside."

Hansel and Gretel followed the old woman into the little gingerbread house, where they were given supper and two very soft beds. Little did they know that the old woman only pretended to be kind, and was really a horrible witch who lured children into her house with sweets.

The next morning the witch dragged Hansel out of bed by his ears and locked him up in a cage.

"I'll have to fatten you up, you skinny boy!" said the witch as she felt Hansel's arm. "And when you're nice and plump, I'll eat you!"

The witch then put Gretel to work. Every day
the girl had to polish the witch's collection of
precious stones, bake the sweets, fetch water, and
scrub the floors.

Every day the witch would hobble out to the
cage to see if Hansel was plump enough to eat.

"Put out your finger," the witch told Hansel.

Hansel knew the witch was almost blind. Instead of his finger, he held out a bone.

"Yeeek!" cried the witch. "You're all bone and no fat! Tomorrow you must eat twice as much!"

But tomorrow came, and again Hansel managed to fool the witch.

Finally the witch lost her patience.

"I can't wait any longer!" she cried. "Gretel, make me a fire and fill the big pot with water. Fat or thin, your brother goes in!"

The witch grabbed Gretel's arm and pinched it thoughtfully. "Hmmm. Let's bake some bread too. Heat the oven!"

Gretel obeyed the witch, trembling with fear. She was afraid for her brother and for herself as well. She suspected that the witch planned to eat them both.

After a while the witch told Gretel, "Check the oven and see if it's hot enough."

Gretel thought for a moment. "I don't know how," she replied.

"Just put your head in, you stupid girl," said the witch. "Like this." The witch hobbled over and poked her head into the oven.

Gretel gave the witch a shove, sending her flying into the oven. She slammed the door and bolted it shut.

Gretel ran outside to free her brother. "The old witch is dead!" she cried. "We are free, Hansel!"

The two children went into the house and filled their pockets with the witch's precious stones. Then they hurried off into the forest, hoping they would somehow be able to find their way home.

The children wandered in the woods for many hours.
They feared that they would never find their way home
when suddenly they heard a voice calling their names.
"Hansel! Gretel! Where are you?"

It was their father's voice!

Hansel and Gretel followed the sound of the voice until they saw their father.

"Hansel! Gretel!" cried the woodcutter. His heart leaped in his chest when he saw his children running toward him. The woodcutter had returned home to find that his wife had died and Hansel and Gretel were missing. He had searched the forest for days looking for the children.

As Hansel and Gretel jumped about with joy, sparkling stones went flying out of their pockets. And just like that, all of their troubles were over.

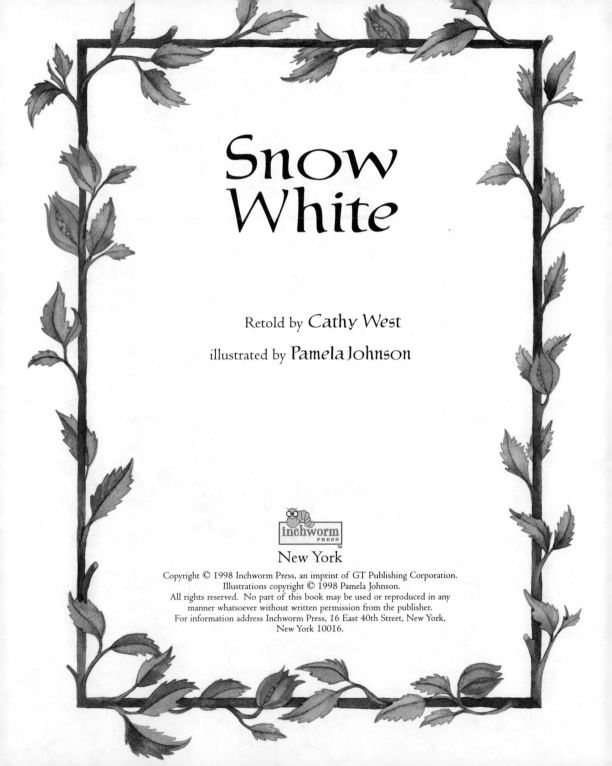

Snow White

Retold by Cathy West

illustrated by Pamela Johnson

inchworm PRESS

New York

Once upon a time, a Queen sat sewing by a window. As she gazed out the black ebony windowframe, she pricked her finger with the needle and three drops of blood fell upon the snow.

"Oh, how I wish I had a child," she said. "As white as snow, as red as blood, and as black as the ebony window."

Soon after, the Queen gave birth to a daughter who was as white as snow, with lips as red as blood and hair as black as ebony. So she was called Snow White.

But then the Queen died.

Soon Snow White's father the King took another wife.
The new Queen was beautiful to look at, but inside she was as
ugly as a witch. Each day she stood before her mirror and said,
"Mirror, Mirror, on the wall,
Who is the fairest of them all?"

And the mirror answered,

   "Thou, O Queen, are the fairest of all!"

And the Queen was pleased, for she knew the Mirror
spoke the truth. But every day Snow White was growing
more beautiful.

Until one day the Queen asked,
    "Mirror, Mirror on the wall,
      Who is the fairest of them all?"
And the Mirror answered,
    "Snow White."
The Queen turned green with jealousy.
How she hated Snow White!

She knew the Mirror spoke the truth.
She called a huntsman into the main hall.
   "Take Snow White into the forest and kill her!"
she ordered.

The huntsman obeyed and carried Snow White deep into the forest. But Snow White was so very kind, the huntsman could not bring himself to hurt her. So he let her go.

Snow White ran into the dark forest. The tree branches
seemed to grab for her, and strange sounds filled her ears.

At last she came upon a tiny little cottage. Tired, hungry,
and frightened, Snow White hurried through the door.

Inside, Snow White clapped her hands in delight. Everything in the cottage was so tiny!

Seven little chairs stood around a tiny little table. On the table sat seven little plates with seven little forks, seven little spoons, and seven little cups. Along the wall, side by side, were seven little beds.

Snow White was so hungry and thirsty! But she did not wish to eat anyone's whole supper. So she ate a little bite of bread from each little plate. She drank a little sip from each little cup. Then she lay down upon the last little bed and fell asleep. Soon the door creaked open. . . .

In walked seven tiny little men. They lit their seven candles and hurried eagerly to the table to eat their supper.

"Who has been sitting in my chair?" exclaimed one.

"Who has been eating off my plate?" cried another.

"Look!" cried a third. "Someone is asleep in my bed!"

The dwarfs crowded around. "What a lovely girl!" one whispered.
Then Snow White woke up. At first she was frightened. But then she
saw that the dwarfs were kind. So she told them about the Queen.

"Would you like to stay with us?" they asked.

"Yes!" she cried. "With all my heart!"

At the castle the Queen smiled and asked,
    "Mirror, Mirror, on the wall,
    Who is the fairest of them all?"
And the Mirror answered,
    *"Snow White—who lives with
    the seven dwarfs in the forest."*

The Queen was furious, for she knew the Mirror spoke the truth. So she disguised herself as an old peddler woman and went to see Snow White. "Apples for sale!" she called out. And she held out a shiny red apple. It looked delicious—but it was filled with poison!

Snow White could not resist. But as soon as she took a bite of the juicy apple, she fell down dead.

The Queen hurried home to her castle and asked,
  "Mirror, mirror, on the wall,
   Who is the fairest of them all?"
And the mirror answered,
  "Thou, O Queen, are the fairest of all!"

The Queen was pleased, for she knew the
Mirror spoke the truth. She knew Snow White
was dead.

The dwarfs wept when they found Snow White. They laid
her to rest in a glass casket so all could see her beauty. And even
the birds came and wept for her.

By and by a prince rode through the forest. When he saw
Snow White in the glass coffin, he fell in love with her.

The prince lifted Snow White up to give her a kiss. The piece of poisonous apple flew out of her throat, and she opened her eyes.

Snow White was alive! The prince begged her to be his wife. Snow White smiled and said yes.

The next time the old Queen
asked her mirror,
"Mirror, Mirror, on the wall,
Who is the fairest of them all?"
The Mirror answered,
"The new Queen, Snow White."

The old Queen was so angry, she never asked the mirror
another thing. For she knew it spoke the truth. And Snow White
and the prince lived happily together for the rest of their lives.